It's Time to Sleep, It's Time to Dream

by **David A. Adler**

illustrated by **Kay Chorao**

Holiday House / New York

Library of Congress Cataloging-in-Publication Data
Adler, David A.
It's time to sleep, it's time to dream / by David A. Adler ; illustrated by Kay Chorao. — 1st ed.
p. cm.
Summary: A parent lulls a child to sleep with visions
of soft spring breezes, lazy summer days, cool autumn winds,
and moonlit winter nights.
ISBN 978-0-8234-1924-1 (hardcover)
[1. Seasons—Fiction. 2. Bedtime—Fiction.
3. Parent and child—Fiction.]
I. Chorao, Kay, ill. II. Title.
III. Title: It is time to sleep, it is time to dream.
PZ7.A2615Its 2009
[E] —dc21
2008022570

For Shira and Greg
D. A. A.

To Sally Nixon Weir
K. C.

It's late.

It's night.

It's time to sleep.

It's time to sleep.
It's time to dream
of drifting clouds,
soft spring rains,
tulips, and daffodils.

It's time to sleep.
It's time to dream,
so close your eyes
and dream of resting
beneath the budding maple tree.

It's late.

It's night.

It's time to sleep.

It's time to sleep.

It's time to dream

of lazy summer days,

sand castles,
seagulls, sailboats,
and ocean waves.

It's time to sleep.
It's time to dream,
so close your eyes
and dream of resting
beneath the shady
maple tree.

It's late.
It's night.
It's time to sleep.

It's time to sleep.
It's time to dream
of cool autumn winds,
mittens, sweaters,
acorns, and pumpkins.

It's time to sleep.

It's time to dream,

so close your eyes and dream

of that maple tree,

its leaves all gone.

It's late.

It's night.

It's time to sleep.

It's time to sleep.
It's time to dream
of cold winter,
star-filled,
moonlit nights,
frost-covered windows,
snowflakes, and snowmen.

It's time to sleep.

It's time to dream

of nighthawks, chipmunks,
turtles, toads,
black bears, and grizzlies,
all asleep until spring.

It's late.

It's night.

It's time to sleep.

It's time to sleep.

It's time to dream,

so dream of me.

I love you so.

Close your eyes,
sweet child.

It's time to sleep.

It's time to sleep.

It's time to dream.